A Saumet

The Gladiator

A Saumet

The Gladiator

ISBN/EAN: 9783337396053

Printed in Europe, USA, Canada, Australia, Japan

Cover: Foto ©Andreas Hilbeck / pixelio.de

More available books at **www.hansebooks.com**

THE GLADIATOR:

A TRAGEDY IN FIVE ACTS,

BY A. SAUMET,

AS PERFORMED BY

SIGNOR SALVINI

AND HIS AMERICAN COMPANY,

UNDER THE MANAGEMENT OF

C. A. CHIZZOLA.

NEW YORK:

J. J. LITTLE & CO., PRINTERS,

Nos. 10 TO 20 ASTOR PLACE.

1886.

THE GLADIATOR.

ARGUMENT.

THE motive of this play is the tyranny of the wealthier and patrician classes of old Rome; the grinding oppression under which the humbler citizens lived; licentiousness, superstition and cruelty which characterized the whole people, and the general atmosphere of hate and revenge that pervaded society. The Christians are introduced to heighten the picture, and a young Christian convert is the victim of the play.

The GLADIATOR is a slave, whose wife has been atrociously murdered by the Empress mother, FAUSTINA. He escapes with his infant daughter. The child is lost. He returns to Rome and visits ORIGEN, a Christian, who lives in the Catacombs. To him he tells the history of his wrongs and announces an intended revolt of slaves. The Empress, with a guard of Lictors, comes to the Catacombs in search of NEODAMIA, a beautiful girl beloved by FLAVIAN, to whom the Empress is herself passionately attached. She misses NEODAMIA, but meets the GLADIATOR. A recognition takes place. The lost daughter's life is bound up by an oracle with that of the young Emperor. The Empress, who has the maternal devotion of a tigress to its cubs, promises reward to the GLADIATOR if he can find his child. Meanwhile she orders him to accompany her to FLAVIAN's palace, where NEODAMIA resides. She orders the GLADIATOR to murder the girl, which he refuses to do.

By FAUSTINA's machinations the marriage of FLAVIAN and NEODAMIA is interrupted. ORIGEN, the Christian, is arrested at the temple of Juno, and NEODAMIA, in a fit of enthusiasm, proclaims her own Christianity. Both are thrown into prison, and sentenced to death in the Arena. The GLADIATOR, who has been held as a runaway slave, is appointed executioner of NEODAMIA. In the Arena he recognizes her as his lost child. He vainly appeals to the people's mercy. FAUSTINA, horrified at her son's danger, involved in the girl's approaching death, adjourns the games, and determines to rescue NEODAMIA, and thereby to ward off peril from her son. NEODAMIA and the GLADIATOR are on the point of making their escape under FAUSTINA's protection, when a riot takes place; the Imperial palace is sacked, the Emperor is slain, and the people, under the guidance of the fanatic Priest of Juno, burst into the prison cells of the Amphitheatre. At this supreme moment, to save his daughter from outrage, the GLADIATOR kills her with his own hand.

Thus the iniquities of the rulers recoil on themselves; and the martyrdom of NEODAMIA gives occasion for the conversion of her father and lover, and for the prophetic denunciation of slavery as a curse upon the nations, to be wiped out in the fullness of time.

ACT I.

SCENE I.

The Catacombs of Rome.—A table of stone with a large open book and a skull.

ORIGEN.

ORI. O, Catacombs! O, temple! sole asylum
Wherein can freely breathe,
Man, oppressed by the cruel yoke of Rome—
That Rome which grows old in bitter
Strife and discord; whose spirit,
That once kept whole the people, now from
Her worn out body dies away. O, Catacombs!
Be your gloom redoubled, the fight
Begins—the future of the world
Is concentrated in one thought, nor doubtful
Is the victory. Tyrants and slaves!
At the great man's foot a people laden
With funereal clothes and chains;
Groans, madness, misery; and of three thousand
Gods, not a single one for the crisis!
Behold thy world, O Rome! behold thy heaven!
But our god has risen, and sheds the ray
Of his light upon his human family.
He whom the entombed spirit makes alive
With its breath, for our eyes can make a sun
And freedom for the soul. Yes! Christ
Our brother,—Christ who was born
On straw, in a manger, sprung
From the common people—but not therefore less
Son to the Omnipotent. In His name
We have fought against a century of blows.
The prisons are with martyrs filled,
The greedy axe gets blunt, in vain
Redoubling its strokes. Alas! we die
On all sides. O, heaven, when shall be erased
From the world's face the scandal,
"That man—can be man's master?"
When? Perchance now, perchance in a thousand years
The sacred tree whose genial foliage

Soothes every pain, will not perhaps
For long ages have spread out
All its branches ; but finally in its
Favoring shelter shall rise matured
The liberty of the world.

.

SCENE II.

NEOPHYTE and ORIGEN.

NEO.	Some slaves
	Are seeking you.
ORI.	I am their protector.
NEO.	Their guide is that Gladiator, of whose
	Victories all Rome used to talk ;
	He has not here been seen these fifteen years.
ORI.	I will move
	Towards them. Wretched slaves. They shall
	Ever have a brother in Origen—to them
	I will speak. The unknown lady
	Introduce meanwhile. Some secret
	To be revealed, has brought her, as she comes
	Into our hiding-place. [*Exit Neo*

SCENE III.

Enter NEODAMIA and NEOPHYTE.

NEOD.	My heart trembles.
ORI.	You are in grief, daughter. Wherefore? The cry
	Of sorrow reaches to us, weak though we be.
NEOD.	And do you console?
ORI.	Our God
	Doth sometimes vouchsafe his healing words by us
NEOD.	One of your sisters seeks
	To throw herself at your feet.
ORI.	Well,
	What shall prevent her?
NEOD.	Fear,
	And—ah, pardon, lord—perhaps remorse
	At her new found joy—

ORI.	She is—
NEOD.	A Christian!
ORI.	Give me then, yourself the confession
	Of that trembling soul ; and I
	Will hear it.
NEOD.	You divine, oh father,
	Her request! A slave by birth, unknown
	Her country or kindred, wherever she
	May turn her feet, she must always have been
	A stranger and an orphan, if Christ
	Had not received her into His family,
	Into His divine mansion.
ORI.	Proceed.
NEOD.	Until to-day, her heart was free and pure
	Of other loves ; but a Roman youth,
	Who yet eternally separated from her,
	Appears by rank in life ; a
	Proud and tender look has turned upon the face
	Of that young girl.
ORI.	(Agitated.) And how?
NEOD.	(Earnestly.) All in honor,
	Not in insult ; respective fully
	Of her jealous dignity. Master
	Of that slave, he seeks to marry her ;
	But....a Christian....He is not.
ORI.	Knows he of what faith
	His slave is ?
NEOD.	He alone in Rome—
ORI.	And she,
	In her new ties, will she to our worship
	Hold faithful?
NEOD.	(Eagerly.) Always! always!
ORI.	Your looks assure me of it ;
	Then take her back this word
	From a priest of the Lord :
	She may, without any peril
	Accept her good fortune. Ever a present help
	Is our religion ; severe she
	Sometimes may be, inexorable never.
	God is not angry at our honest loves.
	Daughter, go in peace.
NEOD.	(O, the ineffable thought!
	Flavian, to be happy—
	And without sin!)

SCENE IV

GLADIATOR and Slaves.

ORI. *to* NEOPH. Admit the slaves.

GLA.   (*Looking around.*) Is this your palace?—So much the
        better!
        Here no pomp offends the light
        Of our eyes. My friends, remain
        In these sepulchral caves. My heart
        Is full already of your grievances—
        For all I speak alone. By the gods!
        Never have I felt so great a need
        Of pouring out my wrath!

ORI.   Be calm!

GLA.   If I lie, may the gods overwhelm me—
        See here—these senses of mine at a mere wink,
        Fly up in flames. So often
        Have I fought the lions, that their roar
        Has got into my voice. Excuse me,
        Master, excuse me. My name
        May be known to you. I am Niger;
        I was born in Thrace; but greater and finer far
        Is my slave name; in Rome I am
        The Gladiator.

ORI.   Among us you will bear
        A name that I prefer to any,
        And most sacred before God.

GLA.   What is that?

ORI.   Brother.

GLA.   The Christians call us brothers?
        Then are all the Christians slaves like us?

ORI.   No, brother; those fetters which pride
        And cruelty invented, fell to pieces
        At the cry of the divine victim.
        Man the slave of man? oh, heaven, what
        Monstrous compact! To God himself
        Man is not a slave. God, who keeps the balance
        Of the world He made, permits evil,
        So that man may be free. So glorious
        In His eyes is that great boon
        Of liberty, that by it alone
        Our souls draw nigh to God.

GLA.   Ha! this is talking! Grand! I like
        Thy doctrine—I love it, and I feel my breast

Expand, and all my vitals
Drink in air by torrents! Thanks, father,
For thy kindness. 1 will pay it back—
Yes, yes! brother. My return to Rome
Is not yet known; I am not wont
To stave off danger—I have staunch friends
Just now to serve; all have sworn
To be revenged for outrage suffered.
We will all lay down our chains together,
Upon the tomb of Rome. All equals,
All oppressed, we offer our heads
To the edge of the sword. You don't know
What it is, to be obliged to cut throats every day;
What it is to swim in your own blood,
When they please to see it; or like us,
To amuse the Arena with our dying breath.
The edict is gone forth.

ORL.   I know it all.

GLA. Help us with your hate. Aid the plot
With your counsel—your great name, and the arm
Of your Christians will be a help to us.
We are ready—all ready.

ORL.   Other arms
Are ours; which make a surer triumph
To the soul.

GLA.   What are they?

ORL.   Prayer and supplication!

GLA. Don't know them! To avenge our long tried
Grievances, there is not blood enough;
And thou offerest tears?

ORL.   As if there were need
Of blood; you, by the brazen foot
Downtrodden, look upon the blood
Of God, which drops from the Cross.

GLA.   Let Him
Fulfil our vengeance, and I will worship Him.

ORL. Brother! who worships this, our God,
Forgoes all vengeance.

GLA.   What say you?—Our
Horrible torments....

ORL.   And what are they to men
Who look upon them with calm aspect?

GLA. Ah! but thou hast not understood me, priest
I am a slave, without a home,

A family, or country ; humbled,
Proscribed, vagabond ; my life worse than a dog's
Tied by a chain, which in some remote
Corner can bite the groom
That lashes him, and vainly
Growling, can work off his rage.   The brand
Of infamy is stamped upon my brow,
Not on my arms or feet, but here upon the brow,
So that the master's mark in the eyes
Of all the world may do dishonor to
The human being all it can.   Oh, what
Store of hate is hidden in this breast,
What cries, what pants for vengeance !
My fate, the Amphitheatre, and Rome
I curse eternally, and insulting,
Spurn this stepmother earth,
That brings forth chains for me ! I insult
And curse that sun, which o'er all the world
Sends forth his light, making more grievous
The air of bondage.   To our gods,
Tyrants that I never see,
I offer defiance as to a fight impossible;
I a dull athlethe ; and vainly on the air
I waste the treasures of my fury.
Revenge misleads me, sweat runs down, my arms
I open wide in the fierce desire
To crush....the universe.

Obi.   What sufferings
You must have had, that your heart gives way
To such a fearful wish.

Gla.   Shall I tell you ?
Priest of Christ you wish to know ?
Listen—'Tis fifteen years ago
Since Faustina was my mistress ; Faustina, now
Styled Empress.   A mother
She was not then ; but to be mother
Desired in heart : whence from those
Who know the future, continually
She inquired, surrounding herself
With wizards and diviners ; and to the gods
Made offerings fitted to appease the furies.
My wife about that time—a fair
Haired Gaul she was—felt the

Trembling of her babe.   Ah ! would she had
Never told it—my hopeful
Pledge of warm enduring love!
But with envious fury Faustina burned ;
And on my wife she looked askance.   One day
While I was dreaming of a happy future,
There came from the palace depths a cry—
A wailing, fearful cry—too well the voice
To me was known—I trembling run.
Ha ! what horror !   Upon a bed of iron,
Pale, naked—my companion lay
On her right side.   With dagger in her hand
A sorceress was saying. " Faustina, you
" Might be a mother, but because the infernals
" Have the power obtained, we must have
" An unborn child, from its mother's
" Womb untimely taken.
" This child, which my art requires
" For its philters, part of its life
" To your son shall give.   Fate to both,
" Whether they be divided or conjoined,
" Will equal make their length of years."
I, with a groan horribly prolonged,
Interrupted the monster.   But the wretch's
Dagger did not flinch—" What do I see ! a man !"
Faustina cried—" It is her husband !   Let him
" Stand opposite and be spectator."
With iron bonds so tightly drawn
That they drew the blood, her Nubian
Cutthroats bound me to a pillar,
Which in my struggles
Fell upon my head, but did not break
My chain ; and then I saw the crime completed—
I saw the victim quiver
Beneath the knife.   There was one long
Mother's shriek—the last.   The heavens did
Not fall ; they did not fall, and dost thou talk of God !
And your child ?

ORI.

ULA.

                The mother was no more :
Faustina's contempt spared the father's
Life.   Night came,
And, torch in hand, I made
My way to the accursed palace.
I gave it to the flames, and from among the ruins,

By hidden ways—with the child, a daughter,
Afar I fled. I saved her
In the desert, in Egypt. I have not told
Half my sufferings ; but nothing more
Is worth the tel.ing.—Now you know what we are ;
You understand the mortal injuries
That men have done me. Is it just
That I wish to exterminate them ? Is it
Not their due ?

ORL   Un'ess you pardon them.
Mercy is heaven-created
In our hearts. Olympus thundered—
Calvary pardons. God chose
To die upon the cross, whence as from on high,
He might extend his arms to all in pity.

GLA.   Pardon them ! I pardon ? Madness.
ORL.   With just such words ever commences
The work of faith.

SCENE V.

NEOPHYTE and same.

NEO.   It is time to
Part. Lictors I have seen
Who violate this gloom that now protects us.
They penetrate the tombs. To execute
Some fatal order they are surely come.
They announce the Empress.

GLA.   Ye gods !
Faustina ?

ORL.   Come, without fear follow me !
Many are the secret hiding places, known
To me only.   (*Exeunt* ORL., NEO. *and slaves.*)

GLA.   I remain.   (*Hides behind a pillar.*)

SCENE V

FAUSTINA, ALBINO, Lictors.

FAU.   Then 'tis truth
You tell me, Tribune. My enemy !
My rival came.....

ALB.   Here.

FAU.   But Christian
        Is not Neodamia.   Are you not mistaken?

ALB.   He cannot be mistaken who has given
        All his mind to serve you.   But by favor
        Of these gloomy labyrinths
        She has escaped our search.

FAU.   And you
        Have not avenged me?   In your hand
        My sword is placed.   You cannot prevent
        This marriage that offends me.   One of them
        Must die.   Too much, Albino, you do delay
        My anger.   I shall before long become
        The Empire's byword.   My wish
        Is known to Rome.   My rank, my name,
        I have forgot for Flavian.—I, the mother—
        I—mother of the Cæsar—they make sport
        Of my anger.   Do not the fools perceive
        In my tears, their death?
        In their insensate love they tender me
        A poison draught—shall I not return to them
        The bitter cup?   We have hearers.

ALB.   No—

FAU.   Yes! see—
        Is not that a man there?

ALB.   Lictors, seize him.

SCENE VII.

GLADIATOR and SAME.

GLA.   To the Empress I will myself
        Advance.   (In the depths of my heart,
        Oh hate, keep still, until shall come
        The auspicious moment.)   I am, I am—

FAU.   I know you.

GLA.   Faustina, guilt
        Keeps memory clear.   What blood
        You needed to write my history—
        Over my heart, my chains,
        My whole life, it has overflowed.—Past
        Are fifteen years, but still 'tis red.

FAU   Slave, to heed thy anger fits me not,
        Where is thy daughter?

GLA.   Where is
Her mother? What hast thou done with her?

FAU.   Away!
What wrong was done? The sorceress
Commanded; I obeyed.

GLA.   Thou obey! Faustina!

FAU.   Yes: it was cruel—

GLA.   Indeed, was it so!

FAU.   After that day
All went ill with me. You may be glad,
However, that in my heart I seem
To be somewhat sorry. The oracle
Was not a liar: I am a mother.
In his three lustres my boy rejoices—
But his father poisoned, and the rebellion—

GLA.   Slave as I am, 'twas not in vain, then, that
I cursed thee.

FAU.   Enough!

GLA.   Given up
By men to anguish, I have yet
Some power.

FAU.   What the gods give thee—

GLA.   And you believe in the gods; and offer them
As best sacrifice....

FAU.   To-day I claim
Thy daughter. Thou art hostage for her;
Know you under what star she is born?
Know you that Cæsar has one fate with her?
That on your daughter the Gods regards are bent,
And sister to the Cæsar
They assign her.

GLA.   Brotherhood Divine!
Cæsar lives, she lives! Meanwhile
She's lost ...to me!

FAU.   Lost?

GLA.   Stolen....

FAU.   She may be restored.

GLA.   Daughter! My daughter!
Clasped in my arms I took her away,
Far away to the banks
Of Nile! and there from every human eye
Concealed I kept her. She slept
Upon my breast by night, and at the dawn we went
To earn our bread. At set of sun

To my blessed cavern home one day
I came—sought everywhere—
It was empty—she was carried away !
Next after thee, this was my greatest grief.—

FAU. And was there no trace ?

PLA.   Long time
I held Osiris' priests suspect ;
They have the rule in Egypt ; I followed
On their tracks ; but finally,
After three lustres of vain fury,
My hands have fallen, and I now despair.

FAU. Thou hast not sought her well. Hear me, slave !
Dost thou not fear my wrath,
Thus putting at guilty risk the days
Of our all highest Imperator?

GLA.   What matters
Your Imperator in my love?

FAU.   Be mindful.
Thou hast lost her, and find her again thou canst,
Beyond all doubt.

GLA.   Oh ! if I could !

FAU.   Well, then,
Go! Recross the sea. Take what gold
Thou wilt, my lictors, and four
Of my galleys.—When found, how
Wouldst thou recognize her?

GLA.   From the day
She first saw light, she has a mark upon her shoulder.
Yes, that very blade that took the
Mother's life·

FAU.   Ha ! I remember
When I checked the current of her blood—

GLA.   Thyself !

FAU. Enough, enough ! Something too much
Of thy laments. In everlasting hate
We should each other abhor, were we not joined
By this tie of offspring. Thus,
I thy child restore.—Thy arm,
If thou succeed shall serve Cæsar,
And thou shalt be free.

GLA.   Free!

FAU.   And rich,
And great—in Rome, or wherever else you please.

GLA. Then like others I shall become a man !

FAU   Thou shalt have titles and property.—

GLA.   And slaves--
       Their bonds to loose?

FAU.   And now depart!
       Go, quick! on duty.   Help
       From Africa's Pro-Consul thou shalt have—
       Temples and palaces carefully explore.
       First, however, I would have thy service
       For a single day.

GLA.   So suddenly—

FAU.   I will have thee secretly into Flavian's
       Mansion find an entrance.   The garden
       Keys I keep myself.   Thou canst have
       Trusty escort.   Destiny has
       Brought thee hither for this purpose;
       But let no one come upon thy traces.

GLA.   Make use
       Of my blade against him.   I have long time sworn
       Hatred and death, to every head
       That rises above its fellows.   Dost thou seek
       Vengeance on Flavian?

FAU.   No; follow me!

GLA.   I follow,   (*She goes off.*)
       Expecting from heaven the happy day,
       When on thy own guilty head I shall have....vengeance!

END OF ACT I.

ACT II.

SCENE I.

Gardens on the Tiber. Statues—Plants—Guests on couches of bronze and mother of pearl inlaid with gold and tortoise shell. A lapis insuli table with fruits and goblets. Boys bearing alabaster or silver jars serve the guests.

FLAVIAN, OCTAVIUS, LUCIUS.

OCT. May the gods keep thy gardens
  Safe from Polar winds! They excel
  Agenor's boasted gardens, by the shade
  They give us. Bring me flowers!
  How I like flowers! Thou shouldst not quite despoil
  Thy porphyry vases to-day
  Delphyra, for us.

FLA.   This is a solemn day;
  More so than you think. I summon you
  As witnesses, my dear friends, to a marriage
  That will change my life for ever.

LUC. Is it a jest?

FLA.   It is no jest.

OCT. What woman so rash that dares
  To press thy hand? Aglae? Many a time
  I shall join the train of her thousand lovers.

LUC. Stella? In luxury will be buried
  Thy every duty.

OCT.   Really I believe
  It is that blond girl, Epicharis.

LUC.   Thou'rt wrong;
  'Tis Julia keeps him in her service.

OCT.   Is it true?
  The Empress?

FLA. (*Angrily.*) No! Among my own slaves
  There is one whom I shall make
  Free before you all.

ALL.   How?—what?—

FLA. Love waits on her perfect virtue!
  To her matchless beauty I have offered

Given, all my heart. Free am I only
Since that day I loved her ! Already full
Of another flame, my soul had been subject
To my senses. Now, not the madness
Of deceptive passion, nor yet the snares
Of joys, on which follows quick regret—
Joys that are but lamps to make more black
The gloom of vice. A love more true,
A love more beautiful in glory....is this
Which Neodamia first excited in my heart ;
That purest countenance, where sadness
Peeps through veiled modesty, shines for me
A star unseen by all the outer world.
The goddess Vesta has come down to make her shrine
Within my doors.

OCT.   Is he turned Nazarene ?

LUC.   Not he ! He is nothing but a—lover.

FLA.   You
Shall be my witnesses, for I will make
My slave my wife. Be not misers
Of a friend's indulgence.

OCT.   Dost thou know
Her ? my friend—

LUC.   Not I !

OCT.   Nor I !

SCENE II.

NEODAMIA and Slaves, *crowned with roses.*

FLA.   Neodamia !

ALL.   How beautiful she is.

FLA.   Draw near ; to-day the feast
Without you, would not be : thenceforth
More lasting be its joys
In your approval.

NEOD.   My lord.

FLA.   (*Introducing her.*) The better part
Of my not many friends.

OCT.   Together bound
By sacred vows.

FLA   Sacred indeed.

Luc.	As those which now are made at your feet.
Oct	With us the ties of friendship bind like oaths.
Neo.	Friendship, I have heard

Binds love itself more closely ; and so I think,
To-day I am assured.

Fla.	And Flavian

Never will deny what she says,
With such a pretty speech.

Luc.	Truly

Happy art thou.

Fla.	Neodamia, your

Lord would make you one request !

Neo.	I attend.
Fla.	He wishes now to see you at his feet—

Command to-morrow.   Obey to-day.

(She kneels before him.)

There is not in all my Tiberine garden
A branch so sacred which can make thee
Free ; as now my noble sword
Thus makes thee free.   *(Touches her forehead with sword.)*
Rise up :
The shame of slavery is wiped away :
Henceforth be free.

Neo.	Your hand

I bless.

Oct.	She knelt a servant

And she rises queen.

Fla.	Now you can

Fly from me, if so you wish : bonds
And masters are no more.

Neod.	Do you think—

You ...Flavian ?

Fla.	No, indeed—I lose a slave,

I find a wife.

Luc.	Friend ! Rome

'Will take exception to this wedding.

Oct.	*(Aside.)* Much more,

The Empress.

Fla.	Wherefore, all Rome

J ask as guests at my nuptials.

Neod.	I expect you

To-morrow at the altar.

Fla.	In Juno's Temple !

3

OCT.	If our eyes be kept on you But little incense will the goddess get.
NEOD.	The incense Of this heart other gods shall have.
LUC.	Receive our farewell.
FLA.	Friends, adieu ! (*Ex.* OCT. *and* LUC.)
NEOD.	My Flavian—my heart did tremble When I named the altar.
FLA.	My little girl !
NEOD.	It sounded blasphemous.
FLA.	What matters The altar's name ?
NEOD.	Oh say not so, To-morrow I will follow thee ; another day Thou wilt follow thy faithful friend In the Christian's church.
FLA.	Your pleasure Shall be done.
NEOD.	Your sacred word Origen shall see. By his binding words We will be worthily united.
FLA.	Hide, Oh hide this fearful secret, Darling mine !
NEOD.	I have promised ; and I will.
FLA.	The name of Christ will else be mortal to thee ; Thy death is mine. The hour Is near when the Emperor expects me For important business.
NEOD.	To instantly return—
FLA.	I return After a little to thy feet
NEOD.	When Flavian Leaves me, with him it seems that all my Happiness takes flight. Pardon My weakness. Adieu. (*Ex.* FLA. Happy ? How happy I am. Why, then, tremble ? And in my secret soul feel Thus agitated ! I feel A need to be alone, with my own Angel. Oh ! let him spread his wings O'er my head and guard me.—Oh, I will

Read with him in this holy book.
This is the law of the Lord, the law
Of a new age.—Incline, ye branches,
Make your shade more dense, ye gardens
Of my Flavian, keep peace and silence
About my footsteps. This is the
Saviour's law. (*Retires.*)

SCENE III.

FAUSTINA and GLADIATOR.

(*During* NEODAMIA'S *speech, they observe her.*)

FAU. I am not mistaken. I see
With my own eyes. The girl is pretty.
Perhaps I thought—— I am not cruel.

GLA. You ?

FAU. Flavian, I would rescue from dishonor.
He is detained just now by Gordian
Through my device ; I have letters—I wish
To act with mercy, that the unhappy one—
My feeble rival,—may open her eyes
On her own folly. If my proofs
Should be in vain, here is a dagger.—Strike
When in my eyes thou readest death.

GLA. I obey.

FAU. It is well. What innocence
She bears upon her face.

(GLADIATOR *retires, but keeps within sight.*)

SCENE IV.

NEODAMIA and same.

NEOD. The Lord is here,
He has heard my prayer.

FAU. Girl !

NEOD. (*Hiding roll in her garments.*)
Ah, my God ! Am I ashamed of thee ? Excuse me,
Lady. I am Neodamia, who are you ?

FAU. A friend till now unknown.
But on my soul, well am I known
To your husband.

NEOD   What say you? As yet
Is Flavian not my husband : but will be
To-morrow.

FAU.   To-morrow? To your
Young lover I will speak, then.

NEOD.   Oh | my
Lord call him rather.

FAU.   This name
Forget forever ; it is a sad one
To remember.

NEOD.   Of all my memories
There is not one which can humiliate me.

FAU.   Very happy are you then.

NEOD.   Oh, God | Happy |

FAU.   Only in hearing you can I understand. So young,
So beautiful.....Come, I love you.

NEOD.   You love me? You?

FAU.   Yes, really |
I know not wherefore, but the love I bear
To Flavian, on his beloved,
All falls back. (Dangerous love
For thy young life.)

NEOD.   Beloved indeed
Is Flavian in Rome, and me who am
His special joy, perhaps they will love
For his sake.

FAU.   Ah, so. His special joy—his—
Who would be but for you? They say
He sets you before the noblest dame
In Rome; they say, but it is late
To repeat it ; for at your feet
Doubtless he has made his boast.

NEOD.   No | lady | And I, when such a heart
Is given me—how could I care
For that he leaves behind.

FAU.   Oh my child,
And so you are not jealous ; I see it.

NEOD.   I jealous | of him |

FAU.   (What triumph
In that look.) Who could ever
With a single word have subdued that heart,
Rebel against love, excepting you
So young, and so—beautiful? My child,
Are you in your sixteenth year?

NEOD.	In my sixteenth.
FAU.	Oh, charming age;
	Ah, adorable youth ! The gods
	Have no better gift for a bride—
	A promised bride! Your glorious marriage
	Occupies my thought—I speak of it
	All day, and dream all night. In Rome
	They talk of nothing else ; in Rome
	You are admired ; in Rome again
	You are blamed and envied—and pitied !
NEOD.	Who should pity me ?
FAU.	Yourself.
NEOD.	' ?
FAU.	Yes ; yourself ;
	Should pity yourself. And I when looking
	On that face serene, those lips
	Of rose, those eyes, and godlike hair,
	Most lovely maid—much in my heart's
	Depths oppresses me—pity.
	Flavian is fickle, and you are
	So tender. Flavian may,
	After incense offered, recklessly
	Throw down his idol.
NEOD.	This speech—
FAU.	In pain all inexperienced
	Is your youthful heart : but admit
	That all is ready for this festivity,
	And weigh with me the value
	Of his conquest. Flavian—
	I know him well. Thou knowest him not yet
	Thou art his wife—I will guide thy steps.
	Before, in this way, before three days
	Are past, no more, thou shall see the end
	Of his constancy. Thou seest not,
	Thou a weak girl, to whom but yesterday
	He gave his heart, that thou canst not
	Make him proud—in thy passion.
NEOD	Alas ! this humble passion he holds dear,
	He is jealous of it, selecting me when
	He might make his choice of many.
FAU.	You force me—you yourself.—All Rome
	Is well informed of his perfidious loves.
	Read this letter, and then answer.
	See, written yesterday. It is his hand.

NEOD. Flavian! oh woe! Thy sister,
Thy betrothed, thy own.
So deceived! Thou!

FAU.   No promise
Is held sacred in his eyes.

NEOD.   Then am I
Lost.

FAU.   No.

NEOD.   Desperate! My God,
What shall I do?

FAU. Fly at all costs : it is needful
To save yourself from this shame
And contempt.

NEOD.   Fly!

FAU.   Yes, from Rome.
Come—

NEOD.   Fly!

FAU.   At all cost. I am
Powerful, Neodamia, and I am your
True, loyal friend.

NEOD.   Ah, you give me terror!

FAU. My arms are open to thee. The heart
In time gets hardened against the ills
We all must suffer. Fly from Rome!

NEOD. Ah, Flavian!

FAU.   Flee from his yoke,
This air is mortal to thee. At every step
A snare may catch thee, at every step
A barrier hem thee in. And there above all
Is thy rival? Ah, thou knowest nothing?
Thy rival—

NEOD.   Unknown to me have ever been
The ways of sin—

FAU.   Thou art a victim,
A needful victim to the pride
Of the offended lady. It needs it must be ;—
That thou give way! Oh, foolish girl! And yet
I open wide my arms again.

NEOD.   Now pitiful,
Now threatening, you who are the safeguard
Of my innocence, you who speak
Of mercy while bringing me death—
Who are you!

FAU. I am thy fate,
Thy judge. I am at this instant
Thy preserver : miserable, tremble
When at last I turn thy Empress.

NEOD. Great Cæsar's mother ?

FAU. And thy rival !

NEOD. Great Heaven !

FAU. Now understand to what dangers
Thy head is here exposed. Understand
If insulted i should be by thy refusal,
What value in my eyes
Had the blood of a paltry slave—
Of a slave who would be hunted o and fro
And trampled under foot : whom none
On earth would dare receive. The kings of the East
Slaughter them by thousands, and for sole cause,
That Heaven may send upon their eyelids
A quiet sleep. Once again
And for the last time I offer thee
My friendship. Fly—Faustina's pity
Lasts but for a moment—
Fly.

NEOD. Flavian must come. I stay

FAU. Under the roof of this unfaithful lover
A betrayer.

NEOD. Of my Lord.

FAU To save thee
I was willing—Niger thou seest—

GLA. I see !

FAU. To him I leave thee—Adieu. (*Ex.*)

NEOD. (*Falling on a marble seat.*) Rise. Be brave,
My soul ! But not so easily arises
The flower crushed and trodden under foot—
Flavian. Flavian—Jealous
Exceedingly is Heaven, and to punish me
Has chosen out my husband. Pain
And sorrow everywhere ; and infamy.

GLA. (*After looking around stands before her.*)
Now we are alone !

NEOD. And then ?

GLA. Poor child ! And I about—
And can you forgive me now for ever !

NEOD. Forgive ?

GLA.   She knows not. I have orders
To slay you, but your voice.
And looks and tears,—

NEOD.   My heart
Has no more tears : take my blood,
That he may find me dead at his return.
I am so wholly wretched.

GLA.   No you are not.
She who armed my hand, chose
To torture your heart before my hand
Should slay you. I have the steel,
She the words.

NEOD.   She lied ?
Tell me she lied.

GLA.   Ah, how she makes me suffer !

NEOD.   You will not kill me now ; oh, kill me not !
I do not wish to die. I ask your mercy ;
At your feet.

GLA.   No to my heart that beats,
Arise—

NEOD.   But that letter ?

GLA.   Long ago
'Twas written—Long ago—

NEOD.   Then he
Loves me still ?

GLA.   He loves thee ; this steel
That hung over thy head is the proof.

NEOD.   Ah, my delight.

GLA.   Poor little one.

NEOD.   Flavian is true. Why then do you
Pity me ?

GLA.   Thy rival,
Cruel, great and powerful,
Is in anger ; Flavian loved her once,
And from her blows to save thy head,
We need a God.

NEOD.   My own God.

GLA.   This Empress frightens me ;
I am afraid of her. I too am a slave.

NEOD.   Your bonds shall be broken, and
Flavian shall do it.

GLA.   My bonds
Are precious in my eyes become. By crime
I could have broken them ; let them stay,

Sublimest badge of honor on my arms.
Flavian—oh, imprudent I close
Your eyes in danger. His glorious
Alliance, alone can be our sh h k
And buckler. Let us return
Within his palace.

NEOD   May heaven protect you.

GLA. Meanwhile the Gladiator is your protector.

END OF ACT II

ACT III.

SCENE I.

Temple of Juno. Statues of Jupiter and Juno.

GLADIATOR and FLAVIAN.

FLA.   Faustina gave you this weapon that in
Neodamia's bosom you should plunge it.

GLA.   She gave it me.
Amid the marriage preparations, a
Secret dagger was prepared for that poor child.
I bring down on my head all Faustina's anger,
But think not of me I my heart, my hand,
Are at your disposal.

FLA.   My Neodamia I In the
Imminent peril, I resigned at once
All dignities with which the empera
Had invested me. Our marriage is hastened
By a day, and secrecy shall protect the rite,
Faustina will not dare
Profane these walls. The priests
Of Juno have meanwhile the charge
Of my affianced, and are well informed
Of my design.

GLA.   These sacred walls
Give no relief to my alarm. Faustina—
You know her not as I do, you have not
Seen that woman's look
When flames of vengeance sweep over
Her fierce soul? Open your eyes
And keep them upon your bride ·
In the hour of danger.

SCENE II.

A TRIBUNE, Lictors and same.

FLA.   What do you
Require, Tribune?

TRL	A Thracian slave.
GLA.	Here I am.
TRI.	In Rome a spectacle is preparing
	For to-morrow, and you are expected
	In our amphitheatre.
GLA	Good. To-morrow
	I will come, Tribune—art thou content ?
TRL	Not at all.
GLA.	No ?
TRL	Thou must follow now
FLA.	His security
	I will be.
TRL	Excuse me.
FLA.	What hast thou to fear ?
TRL	My orders are precise, I may not
	Disobey them.
GLA.	To-morrow—
TRL	The prayer is vain.
	From the Roman people's pleasures these fifteen years,
	Flight has withdrawn you.
GLA.	My flight
	Was all legitimate. By a crime
	Faustina broke my bonds.
TRL	It is of no use.
FLA.	Obey.
TRL	Follow me—
GLA.	In this temple
	There is a right of asylum.
TRL	How ?
GLA.	I will not come !
	At the foot of Jove I wait you, and defy you !
TRL	Right of asylum the temple even of Jove
	Has not for slaves.
FLA.	This is the law.
GLA.	Oh, Jove ! oh, king of gods ! for the unhappy
	Hast thou then no altar ? They persecute me
	Even on thy threshold ! Before the Gods
	Is equality denied—are not mortals
	All one family ? O, Jove ! O, Jove !
	By their offences men accuse
	Thy divinity. To misfortune
	Even prayer is denied. In heaven, as on
	Earth, I proscribed am. My chains
	Divide me even from thee. Infamous laws !

My chains which rather ought
To bring me near to thee.   *(Strikes the statue.)*
     God who art
Already near to falling, god of stone,
Who canst not hear, crush me if you
Cannot defend me, make me free
With death !

TRI.   The circus waits.

GLA.   Let's go. Adieu. Better the lion and tiger
Than such a divinity.   *(Exit.)*

FLA.   The first essay is this
Of the strife that wicked woman wages.
I know Faustina's love ! The weapon
In the slave's hand? and now she punishes him
For his noble refusal. The slave
Shall be free, I swear it.—'Tis she, 'tis she.

SCENE III.

FAUSTINA.

FAU. Answer Flavian. In your own hands
Do you hold the issue of your fate.
Whence comes it that you dare lay down
Your titles and your offices, despoil yourself
Of all your dignity, without asking from me
Or from my son, permission?
I speak not now of my past gifts,
Nor of honors at which Rome has stood amazed.
In Gordian's name you are now commanded
By his mother, that without delay, you
Do assume the honors and the power,
As Proconsul of Gaul. Besides, and herein I yield
To reasons of state, it is the firm wish
Of the entire Senate—I still hesitate—
They wish that from the illustrious names of Rome,
I choose myself a—husband, and that the weight
Of government, too heavy for my son,
Be divided in two parts. Now this election,
You see it well, is no light task.
A husband for me, whose help the Emperor
Invokes, must be great, illustrious and
By Romans honored. My son
As a sacred trust I place

In his hands : and in his virtue
Lies our every future hope.
Your advice, O Flavian, I await :
Speak! I command you

FLA.   What ! you ask
Advice from me? You? I feel the value
Of this distinguished honor.

FAU.   At what preferment
Can Flavian be surprised? And this
Is not the greatest, if he bear in mind
Our kindness and his own glory.
It is not the greatest, if he do not forget
The ties, the solemn ties,
That bind him to the throne. Immense imprudence
Might it be in him, to throw aside the burthen
Of such duty. On the loftiest heights
Of greatness, we take but one step backward
And fall into an abyss.—Now speak :
Say what to-day inspires in you the love—
Of Rome.

FLA. A double Emperor would be
The ruin of the Empire.

FAU.   Does Flavian fully
Understand my wishes? Does he not ——
Does he not make error in the advice requested?
Looked he so high that he could read the name
I destine to protect the Empire.

FLA. The sovereign power should be retained
By Cæsar only.

FAU.   Are the obstacles such
That they are insuperable ?—A refusal
With smiles of derision? How comes
The Empress in this temple? Why comes
She to insult the majesty of the Immortals
With her bold brow? Hear.—By this
Love my shame, on the throne
Of the Cæsars, in this love
Thou mayst reign.

FLA.   Lord of my allegiance
I hold your son.

FAU.   If thou hast listened to yonder slave,
Dost thou not tremble? By what I dared
To punish a rival, judge what I can do
To succeed. The pomp and ceremony

Thou hast come here to arrange for her,
Knowst th u by what torches I could illum'ne is ?
Knowst thou not that this altar whither thy
Offence drags her may change to an altar
Of sacrifice? And that the gods propitiated
For this marriage, may call for blood,
If I make them speak? I know your fame,
I know how dear your name is held
Among the Prætorians, and I know
The power that gives you victory. Ruined
Thou mayst drag me down in thy fall.
The lightning I bring down may burn
Up myself, I know it : but my fall
Would be ruin—
Of the empire. First of all, my rival
Shall descend to the tomb. For one instant
I shall triumph. Shatter a whole empire
For a slave! ! To thee I bend
From the height of the throne. Throw
Away a crown for her !—Forget your
Vows to me, until that hour
When, opening your eyes, you recognize
The awful consequences. Thou hast
Worked thy own ruin, and it is complete
This very day. Wailing and sorrow
For the wedlock done in Rome.

FLA. Monster go—Of thy rage the results
I will not await—For the first time
I have this day felt fear for her. We will fly
Into exile—To our love
Gallia shall be the safe asylum. Who comes?
          (*Wedding procession.*)

SCENE IV.

NEODAMIA, PRIEST of JUNO.

FLA. Neodamia !
PRIEST.   Before immortal ties
Unite two loving hearts in one destiny,
Let us invoke the gods who are protectors.

Of hymen—great Juno and Jove
Tutelars, with those from whom eternal
Rome derives her name.   Before the sacred statues
Let the holy fire—   (*Noise without.*)
            What profane
Uproar disturbs the asylum of the Gods.

FLA.   Heaven—

PRIEST.   The populace in riot advances—

FLA.   Faustina!

NEOD.   Flavian—

SCENE V.

A TRIBUNE.

TRIB.   O priest
Our deities are insulted : before these
Very buildings, a vile Nazarene
Blasphemes.

PRIEST.   A Christian ! A Christian !

TRIB.   He curses our feasts. My
Lictors have him, and bring him to
Your hands.

PRIEST.   His brutal madness
I will confound, Tribune.

FLA.   Finish instantly
The rites commenced. -

PRIEST.   Your marriage
Can I bless on outraged altars
Whence Jove still unavenged   ks down ?
When with impious words the Nazarene—

TRIB.   Let him sacrifice or die—

FLAV.   O my beloved,
Let us retire.

SCENE VI.

ORIGEN in chains, crowd.

TRIB.   Great priest
We transfer to thy avenging God
This sacrilegious Christian.

NEOD.   Origen !

FLA.   Let us go!

NEOD.   O remain, my Flavian.

PRIEST.   They charge
That to-day you have dared to threaten
With your looks this temple.   Is it true?

ORL   Would
The walls fall if I looked at them?

PRIEST.   Pride
Inspires these sacrilegious words.

ORL   Pride is a virtue with thy creed.

PRIEST. See there they bow; do thou too bow
The head.

ORL.   Under the sword—it is ready.

PRIEST. Down in the dust—and worship.

ORL.   Ah! of dust
Indeed thy gods are made—I do not worship!

PRIEST. Dost thou presume thus far in madness
Which to the vulgar seems austerity, to make light
Of earth, the benefice of the gods.

ORL   This obscene fraternity of gods,
Fills your vast temples with people
That destroy each other; profaned
With unlawful incense, your Olympus
Has already crumbled under the enormous mass
Of crime that oppresses this earth.

PRIEST. If it could crumble, on the head
Of your god it would crumble.   Beneath the foot
Mine shall crush him—The day begins,
When thy Christians shall be swept away.

NEOD.   Oh Heaven.

FLAV.   (*Aside.*) Be silent.

ORL   The greatest gain—
For us is death.   Our bodies
Burn, our bones disperse and to your
Executioner give rest,
With all your array of lions.   For
As after a day of fatigue the sense
Gives way to sleep; when it is time to die
The Christian is ready in a moment.
At Thebes, in Asia, in the desert, here
In the dungeon, everywhere the palm
Of death puts forth its flowers: wherever
The seed of martyrdom falls,
It roots, and though death strike us
It raises up the world.—Every Christian
In this glorious race pants

Fervidly, and borrowing help
From death, he runs to victory

PRIEST. Let him be dragged—

NEOD Stop—The funeral palms
Which are made ready for him, see them
Also for his brethren. The scandal
Of a bliss without a risk
They ask not: and for the crown immortal
They lift their heads.

FLA Oh gods !

ORI. What sayst thou '

TRIB. And makest thou common cause with him !

PRIEST. Oh lady, why defend him ?

NEOD. I am a Christian.

FLA. Neodamia !

TRI. Oh, fearful crime !

ORI. Oh, glorious faith !
It is well—I recognize you.

FLA. I defend her !
To free her from thy calumny
My love surrounds her.

ORI If thou lov'st her
Truly, Roman, leave her
Her crown.

PRIEST Thy crown
Is death.

FLA. What hast thou done ?

NEOD. My duty.

ORI Take thy place at my side.

FLA. Oh, rash one.

NEOD. At thy side I see an angel.

PRIEST. Oh, deluded girl !

FLA. Sacred
Is the Roman citizen's family :
She is my wife.

TRI. Incomplete
Was this odious marriage.

FLA. To the altars
Of our deities, before you, did she not come
By herself ? even as I came here
This day to this temple ?

PRIEST. Most true,
She did so come.

FLA.	Do hear ?
NEOD.	Flavian !
FLA.	She is prey

To some hor.   , evil influence, 'tis sure.
It is the forc   spells.

PRIEST.   He says the truth.
O maiden—s.......nce to the gods—
Be free.

FLA.   Thou wilt not quit
My bosom to embrace death ;—
Thou lov... me

NEOD.   Flavian !

FLA.   Love me—O potent
Cry. How sublime love makes the soul !
A word from thy lips, one only,
Conquers them all. Ah ! pronounce it, dear,
Pronounce it. Let our marriage be complete—
Sacrifice—for me, only for me.

NEOD.   Great God,
What ecstacy !

FLA.   Of love! There is the altar
Of our marriage—come, I guide thy heart.
Come, my hand leads thee.

PRIEST.   She advances,
Drawn to the altar by her beloved spouse.

ORL   Her heavenly spouse, to the glorious altar
Of martyrdom calls her !

FLA.   Come, oh come !

NEOD.   I love thee—where am I ?

FLA.   Before the altar.

NEOD.   Before the altar ! oh horror ! I extinguish

           (*Overturns the incense tripod.*)

The incense ; I will meet thee in Heaven.

ALL.   Sacrilege.

PRIEST.   Death and the circus for the Christians !

ORL   The circus when the martyr falls
Is the road to Heaven. Let her follow me.

PRIEST.   Lictors !—

FLA.   Thy fury—

PRIEST.   The circus awaits them.

FLA.   Without arms ? Over my body then—

NEOD.   Adieu.

FLA.   Never ! never !

PRIEST.   Separate them.

FLA   Monster !

NEON   I !   ; lost a husband.

ORL   God will restore thee

        {   ful, redeemed in Heaven.

END OF ACT III.

ACT IV.

The Amphitheatre. The Imperial Balcony. The Priests' place.

FAUSTINA, the PRIEST OF JUNO, GLADIATOR, TRIBUNE, PEOPLE.

TRIB.   The priest is about to speak.

FAU.   There is no doubt
Of my revenge.

TRIB.   Into the arena
The daring Christian will be brought.
Flavian is arrested.

FAU.   I would have it so—
I believe in the gods of Rome. They understand
My wishes.   (*Enter Gladiator.*)

GLA.   Let the lions loose
We shall find each other of one mind.
They are what they seem—let them
Come on. So great an arena,
Romans, pleases the gladiator.
One can fall here stretched at full length.
You have been witness of my glory
And my wounds. My body
Has taken its twenty bites, passing
From tiger to tiger. And now I bring to you again,
After long labors, oh my dear Romans,
Whatever flesh their ferocious teeth
Have left upon my bones. These fifteen years
My nature has not changed: they can
Find on my arms their old
Accustomed food. Let them come, I wait them,
And shall be again triumphant.....Because I wish
To live again, once more to see my child.

PRIEST.   Heaven commands, and in its name I speak.
The daring Christians have violated
Juno's temple. The gods are wroth.
From star to star a cloud of displeasure
Veils Olympus: and upon us now impends
A tempest of misfortune. In vain
The bodies of the sacrifice are opened,
Or smoking entrails studied

With a fearfu' ...ook. Juno is deaf
To the appeal of her priests, and answers not.
Her profaned altars to the care
Of Nemesis are left, until the offence
Be atoned by Christian blood. The games
Are placed under the shadow of celestial auspices—
To the people games, and sacrifices to the Gods
Are given. Between them and Christ, O Romans,
Rages a mortal strife. Wherefore we immolate
A Christian now, and thereby propitiate late.
Let the gladiator strike, and with that blood,
The favor of the Gods, now
By impiety turned aside,
Will fall again on earth.

PEOPLE.   Death
To the Nazarenes!

GLA.   Romans, I shall obey. The head
I bow to the decree of the Immortals. They
Are insulted by the audacious Christian crowd.
The slave's hand shall avenge
The holy gods, and I will punish
The great rebel crime. Still....I must say,
I like to fight with lions, and would
Much prefer it.

SCENE IV.

NEODAMIA is brought on by slaves. The GLADIATOR selects his arms

NEOD.   To thee, O Lord,
Thy handmaid brings a docile heart.
This soil is fruitful when it is watered
With our blood, and may these last battles
Cause new germs of faith to spring for every looker on.

GLA.   A woman's voice....This calls
For all my courage....Ready I was
Indeed for different work.
                        What! Neodamia!
Ye gods! And by my hands! Art thou
Truly Christian?

NEOD.   I am a martyr.
GLA.   And Flavian?

NEOD.   In prison.   Now take
My life, and God will take my soul.

GLA.   Romans, once before I refused
To slay this maiden ...Faustina
Knows it well.

PRIEST.   The people are tired
Of delay.

GLA   When we wish to speak
The people will listen.   Their grace I see,
I know her ; she is not a Christian.

NEOD.   I am.

GLA.   My voice drowns thine!
Spare this victim, and for her
Offer up the executioner.

PRIEST.   Let each
Keep his position.

NEOD.   Mine is best
Of all.

GLA.   For ten, for twenty years
In your amphitheatre and against all
Comers, one against all, I swear
To fight, against all—every day—
You only save her—save her.

FAU.   What means
This lengthy talk ?

GLA.   By the Gods!
I call upon you, Romans, answer.

TRIB.   In the Circus
She must fall.

FAU.   Give her to the Lions
If the slave persists.

GLA.   No! I shall not give
Such joy to Faustina.   Come child,
Come to death.

NEOD.   To life.

GLA.   Bow down!
The blow will be more sure.

NEOD.   (Kneeling.)   O Lord,
Deign to accept me, and from my bosom
Take every thought that is not divine.

GLA.   This cuts me to the soul.   Come now,
Courage my hand—I must remove
This veil. (Touches her neck.)

NEOD   Is there not room

For thy sword?

GLA.   No; I shall hurt thee

Too much.

NEOD.   Pity.

GLA.   I must uncover your shoulders,

Excuse me. (*Removes the veil.*) Oh Heaven.

FAU.   She is beautiful; even

The slave is struck by her.

GLA.   Here, here is a scar—

It is from a weapon, O gods!

NEOD.   Death, death.

GLA.   How willing she is—Where did you get that

Dagger cut on your back—

                    (*She makes sign of ignorance.*)

Your father's name,

              His name?

NEOD.   I never knew it.

GLA.   Never?

NEOD.   No—I was a slave in Egypt;

I have no kindred.

GLA.   Ye gods, ye gods!

PRIEST. Strike, strike.

GLA.   I strike her—My own daughter.

NEOD.   I.

FAU.   His daughter?

GLA.   Mine—my daughter—Open O earth!

Must I kill my daughter? O Heavens

Fall on me—

NEOD.   My father!

GLA.   Daughter—Stolen

From my love; felicity I have so

Craved, lost—a hundred times

I have claimed you from these mutilated gods,

In palaces destroyed, in the mist

Of temples burned; taken unutterly

From thy mother's womb;—and that the

Father's knife—her own father—My treasure!

Oh! people, ye would not have this

Horrid crime completed—This is my daughter!

PRIEST. A slave has no children.

GLA   Ha! It is too much!

I am armed with that eternal right

Which thou deniest; I belong to you 'tis true:

My flesh belongs to your tigers,

That is true but the red hot iron
In your lictors' hand, has eaten
Into my face, it has not burned my heart.
I am her father.

PEOPLE.   No! no!

GLA.   Is there no father
Here among ye? Daughter, perhaps
They would hear thee—Ask pardon
With thy own sweet voice.

NEOD.   Heaven!

GLA.   Silence! be still!—Pity, pardon, Romans!
The gods make you ever greater
Stronger and more happy—They are of marble.
Now Faustina thou knowest what fate
Is bound in hers—Thou hast a son.

FAU.   (*Rises.*)   Silence!
(Fatal Oracle—And thus I miss
My vengeance—My rival—My son.)
Your indulgence—Romans. This wretched
Slave passes his own daughter under
The fatal steel, and every mother
Joins me in asking grace.

PRIEST.   In vain.

PEOPLE.   No! no!

TRIB.   You must yield to the tempest.

FAU.   Faustina yield?

PRIEST.   The sovereign people
In the Circus reigns sole. New and unexpected
Faustina is thy clemency; and against her
Thou hast thyself inflamed me only this day.
She is devoted to the gods.

GLA.   No—Brave people
Triumphant people—Your gods
Require not my daughter's blood.
This sentence in your mouths comes
From the Infernals; it is unjust, murderous,
Frightful—Hear ye!—Once in this
Arena, sprang roaring
From the dens a lion on Androcles,
Androcles had saved the very lion's life
In the desert. The lion
Knew him, and licked his feet.
And you did—what? You saved them both—

> Weeping with pity—slave and lion;
> Both were pardoned—now more cruel
> Would you be again-t a daughter and a father!

NEOD. There is no more hope :

FAU.   Call the Lictors !

PRIEST. To stop this death, is the same
> As to overthrow our altars, crime for which
> This woman ought to fall. Still, while punishing
> Her sacrilege, we may yet accordance
> Make between the rights of heaven and of nature.
> She is thy daughter ? Thus, then, Rome gives
> Thee leave to go, and by another hand
> She shall be offered up.

FAU.   Ye gods !

TRIB.   Faustina !

PEOPLE. Let her die !

NEOD.   Hast thou not heard ? On all sides
> They will have me slain.

GLA. Come down into the arena !
> Come down and strike her. Do you want
> My blood ? Take it. To carry her off
> Let your gladiators come !
> Your leopards, whose thirst
> You slake with blood, to devour her !
> Let them all come—over a father's heart.

>   (*Menaces the people.*)

FAU. People, just victim to your anger
> Is this woman ; but one day's grace
> I will that she shall have. Lictors,
> Take her back to prison—
> To-morrow she shall die !

PRIEST.   Thy word is passed,
> Bethink thee on the gods !

FAU.   I do.

PRIEST.   Faustina, bethink thee
> Of the Roman people.

FAU. (*Aside.*) (The coming night
> Will favor my intent !)

GLA.   My daughter !

FAU. People, till to-morrow !

PEOPLE.   To-morrow !

END OF ACT IV.

ACT V.

SCENE I.

A prison.—Great bronze doors.—Torchlight.

NEODAMIA in the Martyr's Robe.

NEOD.　Alone! alone! This cruel
Kindness should not at least have
Separated child from father. This one day
Given to pity, we could have mingled
Our tears, and even have taken
Share each in others' grief. Oh, mournful
Kindness. Deceitful indulgence!
Flavian! Flavian! Ah, that name
Is blasphemy and makes the hair rise up!
From thee, far from thee,
The Lord gives me a place! O, Flavian—
Oh, my lost love!
My friend, Heaven's
Reward in joy thou would'st have been,
Had'st thou been turned by the spirit's breath.
Yesterday, at thy side, I walked trembling
Under the veil of Hymen,
And the heaving zone,
And had an altar;
Such happiness seldom to the world appears.
The martyr's vestments are less glorious,
But in the change there is prepared
A heavenly crown whose light eternal
Comes from the sanctuary of the Lord.

SCENE II.

FAUSTINA and same.

FAU.　Come forth! we must escape.
NEOD　　　　　You here?
FAU　　　　　Neodamia,
fou whom love hath made my cruelest
Enemy; my rival. Hear me!

But a few moments now remain, one hour,
No more. The people murmur,
Full of suspicion, and demand
Your life.

NEO.   And what tie can
Unite Cæsar to me, the daughter of a slave,
In this day of terror ? What matters
My life or death to Gordian ?

FAU. From thy mother thou wast an untimely
Birth, and a just heaven to
Punish me made its decree, that for
My son and thee there was one fortune,
And for his life and thine should be
The limit equal. The immortal gods themselves....
Oh, blow most cruel ! still fixed
To give me pain, threw into your arms
That only mortal, who held mastery
O'er my heart ; they have torn me to pieces,
Turned my heart to ashes, for now
I am reduced to beg, to supplicate you,
On my knees ; and of all the pride,
The honor, the incense, wherewith the adored
Of Rome was girt, nothing remains
But these bitter tears, and the rack
Of these maternal terrors : now I am nothing,
Nothing but a mother.—Ah, these words,
Do they not reach your heart ?

NEO.   I had no mother.

FAU. Gods ! Follow my steps.

NEO.   No, the anger
Which armed you against her, may arm you
Now against me, so that I may prove unfaithful
To the love of my God, alone, supreme,
The only God I have.

FAU.   And Flavian
Do you not worship ?

NEO.   I love him.

FAU   Well then.

NEO.   I must

Die.

FAU.   Horrid thought ! Die !
Thou die ! And my son ! It cannot be—
Fly, Fly ! I myself have Flavian
Released . he is waiting

To carry you off from all the world. He
Desires none but thee. Slave, follow me
Hurry, come. Too well doth Faustina know
The value of thy flight.—"Tis he!

SCENE III.

FLAVIAN and same.

LA. My Neodamia! my joy!
EO.   You here?
And did you come again to see me?
To see me thus?
FLA.   The people are
In revolt. Let us fly—time presses—
Let my love defend thee.
NEO   Oh, tenderness!
Grievous! terrible!
FLA   Faustina has loosed
Thy chains.
NEO.   But I retain them.
Farewell. I remain to die. God commands,
And I have vowed.
FAU.   Thou hast vowed!
FLA.   Ah, Neodamia,
Grief misleads thee. What God is he,
If his law be such,
That it requires us to abandon
Every joy on earth? Ah, come, come!
NEO. Oh God! and do you conspire together
To my ruin?
FLA.   To thy safety.
FAU.   He is thy husband.
Dost thou hear? Thy spouse. And Faustina
Now makes fast your union; she who
Erewhile stood between and separated you,
Now binds as by an irrefragable knot.
With her powerful hand. Ah! let this
Fateful prodigy persuade—I believe not in the Deities
But I believe in the infernal oracle.
NEO. My father is in prison.
FAU.   He shall
Be released.
NEO.   This is too much happiness—
God will pardon me.

FAU.   Cover thy martyr's
         Vestments with this veil.
NEOD.   Quick, quick.
FLA.   Now to fly—who comes?

SCENE IV.

TRIBUNE and same.

TRIB.   The passage
         Is closed by the crowd. They are breaking
         Into the prison, their leader
         The merciless priest. Do not go
         Until the Lictors have dispersed this
         Maddened mob.
FLA.   In a few instants
         My arm shall disperse them.
FAU.   For the life
         Of this girl, your love is a pledge.
NEOD.   Flavian, Flavian !
FLA.   Keep calm. My sword
         Has never failed.
FAU.   Close those gates
         Of bronze !
FLA.   I return quickly:
         Little fear of the sovereign people
         Have our Lictors. At the clash of arms
         Their power falls.   (Exit Fla. and Trib.)
FAU.   The entrance is closed.
NEOD.   He will save me ! It is not the
         People's fury, 'tis God who summons me !
FAU.   No, no ! banish fear ; if Flavian
         Fights, it is for thee ; over all the mighty gods,
         He would be victor. This moment
         Thy marriage is accomplished. Be generous !
         Let my son be safe, and at every cost
         Thou shalt be happy.   (Crash of falling masonry.)
NEOD.   Do you hear ?
FAU.   A wall is falling !
NEOD.   Great heaven !

SCENE V.

The GLADIATOR springs in from the breach.

GLA   I am here !

NEO.   Now I can fly from death,
If I fly with thee!

GLA.   Curses!   •
It is a short-lived joy! From thy face
Strip off that vail. It is useless,
My daughter—useless—my darling child!

NEOD.   Why?

FAU.   Our flight is at hand.

GLA.   What makes
It safe?

FAU.   I myself.   .

GLA.   Too late! Too late!
The prisons are forced, the Lictors'
Eagles have gone down, and
The revolt succeeds everywhere. I, myself saw
The howling torrent of the furious
Populace shrieking
For the Christian victim: the priest
With brutal fury heads them.

FAU.   Oh, terror!

GLA.   My prison, child, is near to thine;
The grating that permitted light
To fall upon my fetters, I tore out,
And creeping through, I fell—
And found myself face to face
With a tiger; I fought him - this dagger
Killed him—I was almost smothered
In his blood. The hole
Begun in the wall by the beast's
Claws, I enlarged enough
To pass me through;
And in this second cell I find myself.
.But what's the use? What can I do,
Save die with thee?

FAU.   And my Tribune!

GLA.   Dead,
Before me!

FAU.   My soldiers, Lictors,
Slaves.

GLA.   What good are they with the rabble
Roaring at the doors, and all the passages
In their power?

FAU.   But Flavian fights:
He can defend her. Then in
My palace——

GLA.   Thy palace is ashes—

FAU   Heavens !

GLA.   The revolt reached there !
    The flames went up, I saw them.

FAU.   Ye gods !
    And my son !—Let us run—

GLA.   Thy eyes, O, Faustina,
    Are open now ; the flames of thy palace
    Have lighted up the prison.

FAU.   This door ?

GLA.   Is shut !

FAU.   Shut ? Oh yes ! but this—

GLA.   Tigers and lions,
    For thy games !

FAU.   And this ?

GLA.   Shut too.

FAU.   Oh, vain and impotent gods !

NEOD   Ah, thou hast driven Jesus away.

GLA.   Daughter, to my heart. No one hast thou who
    Loves thee as I do.

NEOD   Then it is time to die.

GLA.   'Tis the only blessing left.
    Oh, daughter, mine, thy slave father's love
    Is nothing worth. It is but an added blight
    To thy young life. Thou art proscribed,
    Not debased.

NEOD.   Thy fetters
    Make thee dearer to my love.

GLA.   So—
    I love thee—and thou? Happiness I never
    Hoped. The one single joy
    That has come to thy father since the day
    Thy mother died !

FAU.   (*Furiously.*) And these gates
    Of bronze, oh, rage ! Why can they not be opened

NEOD   She is not a Christian. How she must suffer.

FAU.   What horrid danger waits
    Upon my son ?

GLA.   Thy son, sayest thou ?
    And my daughter ? Hast thou forgotten
    That she is of thy family, and that both
    Have one fate, one life—
    And one death ? What did'st thou

Seek? Useless wickedness,
Thy Cæsar's soul in a poor slave's bosom !

FAU. How bitter
Now is the memory of that offence.

GLA. Ah! look
For an instant with a mother's eye
Upon my daughter—young—beautiful,
Only sixteen !

FAU. Horrible! woe, woe !

GLA. Her martyr vesture lies heavy
On the Emperor. Vile and stained
By his mother's wickedness ; on the shoulders
Of thy son the purple will not last
Longer than this black veil—
Cæsar already !——

FAU. Mercy ! Every word of thine
Is as a dagger thrust ! Mercy !

GLA. Hast thou
Ever shown mercy? No ! Cursed
Be Cæsar and the Crown. In my rage
I curse that son
That thou shalt never see ; I curse
That son imperial, over whom
Weighs that solemn anathema which
Would be too awful for a slave !
This diadem on my daughter's front
Would be the circlet of death.

NEOD. Nay, a crown
Of light. Oh, cease, my father,
To profane the holy palm prepared
By the Lord for me. Thy cruel words
Will but recoil on thee.

GLA. What import to me?
My days—

NEOD. On me they will recoil.
(*Outside.*) (Death !)

GLA. No more they call the father,
No more the athlete's mighty arm. Now they
Want my soul : to throw my daughter
To the ravenous tigers. Thy garments
Torn to pieces, will be steeped in blood ;
And ere thou shalt taste death,
Thou wilt have passed through infamy.

NEOD.   Oh, God! Death—
Death first! Thou wilt not see it—

GLA.   No, no!
I love thee too much. Thou shalt see a proof—
Virginius did it once! My courage,
Perhaps, is less than his. What greater
Proof of love—my heart is torn
With rage. Oh, daughter, mine, keep calm,
Utter no cry of horror; let not a word
Of grief escape, nor move an eye
Nor lip, lest I should hear; ah, nothing—
Nothing for pity's sake, my very heart is closed,
      (*Cry without.*) (*Death to Cæsar.*)

FAU.   To Cæsar!
GLA.   Faustina.
Death to Cæsar? Dost thou hear?

FAU.   My son.
GLA. The people want him! For once
They are just. Dost thou hear
And not turn pale? The oracle foreknew;
It is going to be fulfilled.

NEOD.   Hide me
In thy arms, my father.

GLA.   My love is frightened!
NEOD. Will they drag me thence?
GLA.   Yes; but not alive. Oh, excess
Of tenderness.—Oh fury. Ever art thou
The gladiator's refuge—thou only—and always
A despairing fury.

NEOD.   Will they come to
Disgrace thy daughter? God will not have me
Then in his family. Is that so, my father?

GLA. If God protects thee, let him take my place
And save thee. A miracle.   (*Kneels.*)
     (*Cries without.*) (To the lions—
The Sacreligious.)

GLA.   Arise! I alone
Defend thee, I alone. I cannot strike—
Don't look at me.

FAUD.   They come. I hear
Their footsteps. What to do?

NEO.   Save me, my father.
GLA. Save thee from what?

NEOD	From their vengeance--
	This is pity. In face of dishonor
	Death is not seen.
GLA.	Then God
	Leaves me judge of thy fate.
NEOD.	Ah, my father!
	Here, thou art his image.
GLA.	So—so—
	I have my steel. Fear not, thou canst not
	Be torn from my heart.
NEOD.	Forgive,
	Forgive him, Oh, my God!
GLA.	(*Dagger in hand.*) My daughter, embrace me!
FAU.	See, see.—Is hope quite gone :—Heaven,
	What dost thou ?
GLA.	Thus killing my daughter, I prove
	Myself her father. Let her be free. (*Strikes her.*)
FAU.	Celestial gods.
NEOD	I die.
FAU.	Thy own daughter ?
GLA.	And thine.—Let the
	People come, and take her. (*Doors broken open.*)

LAST SCENE.

FLAVIAN, People.

FAU.	Flavian;
	Cæsar, my son ?
FLA.	Dead, before
	This door—wounded—covered with blood !
FAU.	Dead?
FLA.	Thy daughter ?
GLA.	Dead !
	Yes, by my hand; oh, vile, infamous rabble !
PEOPLE	The Gladiator !
FAU.	My son !
FLA.	Neodamia !
NEOD.	(*Opens her eyes.*)
	Ah, thy hand upon my heart. Thou art—
	I see thee really ? Reunited by
	God Himself.
FLA.	And with thee I adore Him.

NEO.	One only God—thy soul—	(*Dies.*)
FLA.	She is dead—ye gods!	(*Kneels.*)
GLA.	I offer up her blood,	

Her martyrdom, and my own martyrdom, to the
Poor and naked god.   And may this steel
Recall to mind what atrocious crime
Has frightened these our times; and flashing
Lightnings in the eyes of tyrants, may it say
To the new age—" Ended is the reign
Of brutal force!   There is no slave in all the world!"

THE END.